MONSTER AND Frog

And the

HAUNTED TENT

For Ben
R.I.

To Archie Harold with love,
Harold and Jeannie

Consultant: Prue Goodwin,
Lecturer in literacy and children's books,
University of Reading

ORCHARD BOOKS
338 Euston Road, London NW1 3BH
Orchard Books Australia
Hachette Children's Books
Level 17/207 Kent Street, Sydney NSW 2000

First published in Great Britain in 2006
First paperback publication 2007

Text © Rose Impey 2006
Illustrations © Russell Ayto 2006

A CIP catalogue record for this book is available from the British Library

ISBN 1 84121 538 4 (hardback)
ISBN 1 84362 229 7 (paperback)

1 3 5 7 9 10 8 6 4 2

Printed in China

MONSTER AND Frog

And The

HAUNTED TENT

ROSE IMPEY ✒ RUSSELL AYTO

ORCHARD BOOKS

Monster and Frog are going
camping.

Monster has never been
camping before.
It is Frog's idea.
Frog is full of ideas.

"It will be a real adventure," he tells Monster. "Sleeping on the ground, under the stars."

Monster does not like the
sound of that. Monster likes
his big soft bed.

Monster drives the car while Frog
reads the map.
They drive for miles and miles.

Monster thinks they have passed
this signpost before.
He thinks they may be lost.

But Frog says, "Do not worry,
I know all about reading maps."

At last, Frog says, "Stop the car!
This is the place."
"Are you sure?" says Monster.

It looks like a big lonely field.
"Trust me," says Frog. "I am
an expert on camping."

First they must put up the tent.
Monster has never put up
a tent before.

But Frog says, "Leave this to me.
I will have this tent up in no time."

The tent *is* up in no time.
But very soon it falls down.
It falls on Monster's head.

Frog tries once more to put up
the tent.

But the tent falls down again. This time it falls on Monster's tail.

"Hmmm," says Frog. "Tents are not as easy as they look."

At last the tent is up.
It is very dark and now it
is raining.

"Time for bed," says Frog.
But there are no beds. Just
sleeping bags on the ground - in
a puddle.

Monster wishes he was at home
in his big, soft bed.

"What an adventure!" smiles Frog.
But Monster does not really
like adventures.

He thinks camping is a bit scary.
Nothing scares Frog. "Lights out,"
he shouts. "Sleep tight."

Soon Frog is fast asleep
and snoring.

But Monster is wide awake.

He can hear noises: snuffling, snorting, chewing noises. It sounds as if *something* is trying to eat the tent.

Monster turns on the torch.
He can see shadows outside.
Big, scary shadows.

"F-f-frog! P-p-please wake up,"
begs Monster.

But Frog will not wake up.
"Go back to sleep," he yawns.

Suddenly, the tent starts to move.
"Help!" whispers Monster.
"Someone is stealing the t-t-tent."

24

Now Frog is awake.

"Go away!" he shouts.

"Stop shaking our tent."

25

The tent stops shaking.
It is very quiet again.

"What if it was g-g-ghosts?"
Monster whispers.

Frog does not really believe in ghosts.
"Leave this to me," he says.
"I will investigate."

It is very dark and creepy outside.
Things are moving in the trees.

Frog starts to think, what if it
is g-g-ghosts?

He hurries back into the tent.
"I have had a good idea," he tells
Monster. "Why don't we go home
and sleep in our own beds?"

Monster likes that idea. He thinks
it is the best idea Frog has
ever had.

They pack up the tent - very
fast - and jump into Monster's car.

"Next time," says Frog, "we will try a caravan. Now, caravans are my speciality."

MONSTER AND Frog

ROSE IMPEY ✦ RUSSELL AYTO

Enjoy all these adventures with Monster and Frog!

Monster and Frog and the Big Adventure
ISBN 1 84121 536 8
Monster and Frog Get Fit
ISBN 1 84121 542 2
Monster and Frog and the Slippery Wallpaper
ISBN 1 84121 540 6
Monster and Frog Mind the Baby
ISBN 1 84121 544 9
Monster and Frog and the Terrible Toothache
ISBN 1 84121 534 1
Monster and Frog and the All-in-Together Cake
ISBN 1 84121 546 5
Monster and Frog and the Haunted Tent
ISBN 1 84121 538 4
Monster and Frog and the Magic Show
ISBN 1 84121 548 1

All priced at £8.99

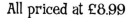

Orchard Colour Crunchies are available from all good bookshops, or can be ordered
direct from the publisher: Orchard Books, PO BOX 29, Douglas IM99 1BQ
Credit card orders please telephone 01624 836000
or fax 01624 837033 or visit our Internet site: www.wattspub.co.uk
or e-mail: bookshop@enterprise.net for details.

To order please quote title, author and ISBN
and your full name and address.
Cheques and postal orders should be made payable to 'Bookpost plc.'
Postage and packing is FREE within the UK
(overseas customers should add £1.00 per book).

Prices and availability are subject to change.